1853
Marie-Grace
MAKES A DIFFERENCE

BY SARAH MASTERS BUCKEY

ILLUSTRATIONS CHRISTINE KORNACKI

VIGNETTES CINDY SALANS ROSENHEIM

★ American Girl®

The American Girls

1764

Kaya, an adventurous Nez Perce girl whose deep love for horses and respect for nature nourish her spirit

1774

Felicity, a spunky, spritely colonial girl, full of energy and independence

1824

Josefina, a Hispanic girl whose heart and hopes are as big as the New Mexico sky

1853

Cécile and Marie-Grace, two girls whose friendship helps them—and New Orleans—survive terrible times

1854

Kirsten, a pioneer girl of strength and spirit who settles on the frontier

1864 · ADDY, a courageous girl determined to be free in the midst of the Civil War

1904 · SAMANTHA, a bright Victorian beauty, an orphan raised by her wealthy grandmother

1914 · REBECCA, a lively girl with dramatic flair growing up in New York City

1934 · KIT, a clever, resourceful girl facing the Great Depression with spirit and determination

1944 · MOLLY, who schemes and dreams on the home front during World War Two

1974 · JULIE, a fun-loving girl from San Francisco who faces big changes—and creates a few of her own

Published by American Girl Publishing, Inc.
Copyright © 2011 by American Girl, LLC

Questions or comments? Call 1-800-845-0005, visit **americangirl.com**,
or write to Customer Service, American Girl, 8400 Fairway Place,
Middleton, WI 53562-0497.

Printed in China
11 12 13 14 15 16 LEO 10 9 8 7 6 5 4 3 2 1

All American Girl marks, Marie-Grace™, Marie-Grace Gardner™, Cécile™,
and Cécile Rey™ are trademarks of American Girl, LLC.

This book is a work of fiction. Any similarity to real persons, living or dead, is coincidental
and not intended by American Girl. References to real events, people, or places are used
fictitiously. Other names, characters, places, and incidents are the products of imagination.

Profound appreciation to Mary Niall Mitchell, Associate Professor of History, University of
New Orleans; Sally Kittredge Reeves, former Notarial Archivist, New Orleans; and
Thomas A. Klingler, Associate Professor, Department of French and Italian, Tulane University

Among the many sources of historical background the author used were *Sword of Pestilence:
The New Orleans Yellow Fever Epidemic of 1853* by John Duffy and *The Diary of a Samaritan*
by William L. Robinson. The author would also like to thank the wonderful
New Orleans museums and guides who help history come alive.

PICTURE CREDITS
The following individuals and organizations have generously given
permission to reprint images contained in "Looking Back":
p. 73—Smithsonian Institution, National Museum of American History;
pp. 74–75—© Bettmann/Corbis (street scene); Mary Cassatt, American, 1844–1926,
The Child's Bath, 1893, oil on canvas, 100.3 x 66.1 cm (39½ x 26 in.), Robert A. Waller Fund,
1910.2, The Art Institute of Chicago (woman and child); Smithsonian Institution, National
Museum of American History (leeches jar); pp. 76–77—University of Arizona College of
Pharmacy (show globe); © Bettmann/Corbis (detail) (traveling doctor); courtesy of the
Library of Congress (Hamlin's Wizard Oil); Smithsonian Institution, National Museum of
American History (bottle of Magic Oil); from the British Columbia Medical Association
Medical Museum (medicine kit); pp. 78–79—Time & Life Pictures/Getty
(Florence Nightingale); North Wind Picture Archives (vaccination).

Cataloging-in-Publication data available from the Library of Congress

FOR JAY AND JEN

In 1853, many people in New Orleans spoke French as well as English. You'll see some French words in this book. For help in pronouncing or understanding the foreign words, look in the glossary beginning on page 80.

TABLE OF CONTENTS

MARIE-GRACE'S FAMILY AND FRIENDS

MARIE-GRACE'S FAMILY

PAPA
Marie-Grace's father, a dedicated doctor who is serious but kind

MRS. CURTIS
A no-nonsense widow who is the Gardners' housekeeper

MARIE-GRACE
A shy, caring girl who is happy to be back in New Orleans

UNCLE LUC
Marie-Grace's uncle, who is a Mississippi River steamboat pilot

ARGOS
Marie-Grace's dog, who is her constant companion

MADEMOISELLE OCÉANE

A French opera singer who is engaged to be married to Uncle Luc

CÉCILE REY

A confident girl who is Marie-Grace's first real friend

SISTER BEATRICE

A warm and wise nun who is in charge at Holy Trinity Orphanage

LAVINIA HALSWORTH

A wealthy girl who likes to be the boss

CHAPTER
ONE
—

SO MANY ORPHANS

September 1853

It was almost noon on one of the hottest days of the summer. Marie-Grace Gardner felt the sun burning her face as she looked around the noisy courtyard of Holy Trinity Orphanage.

Where is Cécile? Marie-Grace wondered. She and her friend, Cécile Rey, were both volunteers at the orphanage. They were supposed to meet this morning, but Cécile had not yet arrived—and she hadn't sent a message, either.

Despite the heat of the day, Marie-Grace felt a chill of fear. Cécile's older brother, Armand, had been very sick with yellow fever. Armand was recovering, but the family's maid, Ellen, had died of the fever. *What if Cécile is sick now?* Marie-Grace worried.

Yellow fever was spreading all over the city. In just three months, thousands of people had fallen ill with the deadly fever. Marie-Grace's father, Dr. Thaddeus Gardner, said that so many people were suffering from yellow fever that there was an epidemic—the worst ever to strike New Orleans.

Because of the epidemic, Holy Trinity was now overflowing with orphans. Some children were running and playing tag in the courtyard, but many others sat in the shade by themselves. Some held tight to their sisters or brothers as if they were afraid to lose what little family they had left.

A little boy with sad brown eyes tugged at Marie-Grace's arm. The boy was new to the orphanage—one of the many children who had recently lost their parents to the fever.

Marie-Grace smiled at him. "Hello," she said. "What's your name?" He stared up at her questioningly, and Marie-Grace realized that he did not speak English. She asked again in French.

"Pierre," he answered. His voice was barely above a whisper. He pointed at the two wooden swings that hung from a tree just a few feet away.

Marie-Grace nodded and held out her hand to the boy. They walked over to the tree, and she helped him up onto one of the swings. "Get ready, Pierre. *Prépare-toi!*" Marie-Grace gave his swing a push, and it arched up into the cloudless sky.

"I want to swing, too!" cried Katy, a little girl who had been at the orphanage for almost a year. She scrambled up on the other seat, and Marie-Grace pushed her swing with both hands.

Katy rode upward, her coppery brown braids streaming out behind her. "Look at me, Marie-the-Great," she cried, calling Marie-Grace by the nickname that many of the orphans thought was her real name. "I'm flying!"

As the sun beat down, Marie-Grace alternated between Pierre's and Katy's swings, pushing each in turn. Pierre was silent, but Katy kept calling, "Push me again, Marie-the-Great!"

Suddenly, Marie-Grace heard another voice calling her name. She turned and saw Cécile hurrying across the orphanage courtyard. Cécile's dainty parasol shielded her face from the sun, but she looked as hot and worried as Marie-Grace felt.

"Thank goodness you're all right!" exclaimed Marie-Grace. She was so relieved that she hugged her friend before Cécile had a chance to put down her parasol. "How is Armand?"

"He's much better, thank you. And I'm sorry I'm late—Maman needed my help filling baskets for the sick," Cécile said breathlessly. "What have you heard about Mademoiselle Océane? Is she better?"

"I don't know," admitted Marie-Grace, and she felt the chill of fear again. "I keep hoping for news from Uncle Luc, but I haven't heard anything since I saw you for the special day of prayer."

Three days ago, people throughout New Orleans had gathered in churches, synagogues, and other places of worship to pray for those who were sick with yellow fever. Marie-Grace and Cécile had been among the crowds at St. Louis Cathedral. The two girls had prayed together for Mademoiselle Océane, their friend and singing teacher. Mademoiselle Océane had planned to marry Marie-Grace's Uncle Luc this summer. But now Mademoiselle was sick with the fever—and Marie-Grace was very worried.

"I'm sure your uncle is with Mademoiselle," Cécile reassured her. "My maman hardly left

Armand for a moment when he had the fever. And we all took turns sitting with Ellen, too, until . . ." Cécile did not finish her sentence.

The girls were both silent for a moment. Marie-Grace understood how terrible sickness could be. Four years ago, her mother and her baby brother, Daniel, had died in a cholera epidemic in New Orleans. Soon afterward, Marie-Grace and her father had left the city. They spent several years moving around the Northeast, but they had never found a true home. Marie-Grace had been glad when she and Papa returned to New Orleans in January. But once again, it seemed as if sickness was threatening her whole world—and her friend's world, too.

Marie-Grace touched Cécile's arm. "I'm very sorry about Ellen," she said gently.

"I can't believe she's gone," Cécile said sadly. Then she looked at Marie-Grace with fierce determination. "We have to find some way to help Mademoiselle Océane."

"I've been thinking that, too," Marie-Grace agreed. "But I don't know what we can do."

"There must be *something*," Cécile persisted. "What does your papa say?"

Marie-Grace gave Katy's swing another push
while she tried to think of how to answer. Cécile had
a big, loving family, and she always had lots of people
to talk with. Marie-Grace wondered how she could
explain to her friend that, for the last few weeks,
she'd hardly seen Papa at all. He had been too busy
taking care of yellow fever patients.

"Papa works every day from early in the
morning till late at night," Marie-Grace said at last.
She pushed Pierre's swing. "He doesn't have much
time to talk."

Cécile nodded. "He stayed at our house all night
taking care of Armand. He has many patients to visit,
doesn't he?"

"Yes," said Marie-Grace, thinking of how tired
her father had looked that morning. "And all he said
about Mademoiselle Océane is that we should pray
for her. I think Papa's worried."

Ding! Ding! Clanging filled the courtyard. Sister
Beatrice was ringing the bell to announce the midday
meal. As soon as Katy heard the sound, she jumped
from her swing. Pierre, however, looked confused.

"Come with us," Marie-Grace told Pierre in
French as she helped him down from his swing.

She and Cécile led him to a big basin in the corner
of the courtyard. There, all the
children gathered to wash their
hands and faces before rushing
inside.

"I'm glad you girls are here to
help," Sister Beatrice told Marie-
Grace and Cécile as they followed the children
into the dining hall. "We've had twenty-seven new
children arrive this week. That's more than we
usually have in a whole year."

So many orphans! thought Marie-Grace as she tied
an apron around her waist. Children ranging in age
from toddlers to five-year-olds sat crammed together
on the benches. Many squirmed eagerly as they
waited for their dinners.

In the far corner of the room, nuns spoon-fed
children who were too young to eat by themselves.
One of the little boys had curly dark hair, and he
reminded Marie-Grace of Philip, the baby who had
been left outside her father's office a few months ago.
Marie-Grace had brought Philip to Holy Trinity, and
she had often come to the orphanage to play with
him. It had broken her heart when he'd been taken to

an orphanage in Chicago. But now she said a silent prayer of thanks that Philip was safely away from yellow fever.

Sister Beatrice handed Marie-Grace and Cécile baskets of delicious-smelling warm bread. "If there is any extra, give it to the new children," she said quietly. "Some of them haven't had much to eat in a long time."

"Yes, Sister," the girls said together. Food was getting harder to find in the city. Some of the ships that brought supplies to New Orleans were now avoiding the port because of the fever. There were empty stalls in the markets, too, and many bakeries and shops were closed because their owners had fled the city.

"We'll make sure everyone gets enough," Marie-Grace promised.

For the next hour, she and Cécile passed out bread and scooped red beans and rice from big iron pots. When the meal was over, the orphans stayed inside for their afternoon rest. Marie-Grace and Cécile went outside and sat under the shade of a magnolia tree at the far end of the courtyard.

"All these children without parents," Cécile said

wearily. "I wonder what will happen to them."

Marie-Grace had wondered the same thing. She remembered how lonely she had felt after her mother died. "Even if the orphans go to live with other relatives, it won't be the same as their real homes."

"No," Cécile agreed slowly. She spread a carefully pressed cloth napkin on the ground. "But when Tante Tay came to live with us, she said that home isn't just one place. It's wherever you have family and friends."

For a moment, Marie-Grace didn't say anything. She thought about all the times she and Papa had moved. Even though they had been together, no place felt like home the way New Orleans did.

Cécile took a flask of lemonade, some bread, and several plump figs from her basket. "Aren't you going to eat something?" she asked Marie-Grace.

Marie-Grace shook her head. She was so worried about Mademoiselle Océane that it was hard to think about eating. Even though Mademoiselle was not yet her aunt, she had treated Marie-Grace like a favorite niece. Marie-Grace remembered the many happy times they'd had together, singing, talking, and sipping tea.

What if Mademoiselle doesn't get better? worried Marie-Grace. Her stomach twisted in a knot when she considered the possibility. *It would almost be like losing Mama all over again,* she realized.

"I'm not hungry," she told Cécile.

Cécile didn't seem surprised. "When Armand was sick, I forgot to eat sometimes," she said as she tore her bread in half. "But Maman said I had to stay strong so that I could help Armand. And I did help him. I sang to him when he was sick, and it made him feel better." Cécile handed half her bread to Marie-Grace. "Here, you have to stay strong if you're going to help Mademoiselle."

The bread felt dry in Marie-Grace's mouth, but Cécile insisted that she have some figs, too. After a few bites of food and a long drink of lemonade, Marie-Grace began to feel a little better.

Cécile picked up a late-blooming magnolia flower that had fallen on the ground. "Look at this," she said, holding up the sweet-smelling blossom. "Wouldn't it be perfect for Mademoiselle's wedding?"

There may not even be a wedding now, Marie-Grace thought. But she couldn't bring herself to say those words aloud.

"I think I have an idea for how we could help Mademoiselle," Cécile said slowly.

Marie-Grace sat up straight. "You do?"

"Yes! We could plan the wedding," said Cécile. "And when Mademoiselle gets better, everything will be ready."

Marie-Grace was disappointed. *Wedding plans won't help Mademoiselle get well,* she thought. She slumped back down on the grass and watched a line of ants scuttle by. "I want to do something for Mademoiselle *now,*" she told her friend.

"Well," said Cécile, "as soon as Armand's fever broke, he started talking about a picture he'd been painting before he got sick."

Marie-Grace looked up from the ants. She knew that Cécile's brother had studied in France, and Cécile had said that Armand was a great artist. "But Mademoiselle isn't a painter. She's a singer," Marie-Grace reminded Cécile.

"I know, but Armand says that just *thinking* about finishing the picture gives him something to look forward to," Cécile explained. "Don't you think Mademoiselle would like to think about her wedding?"

"I think I have an idea for how we could help Mademoiselle," Cécile said.

Marie-Grace shrugged halfheartedly. But then Cécile started to tell her about a fancy wedding she had been to once. Cécile described the church, the music, and the bride's elegant gown with such detail that Marie-Grace couldn't help getting caught up in the story.

"The bouquets were as tall as—" Cécile grabbed her parasol and lifted it high above her head "—as tall as this! They were the most beautiful flowers I've ever seen."

"Mademoiselle might like that," Marie-Grace admitted.

"Of course she would!" said Cécile confidently. "I'll ask my maman if we can use some flowers from our garden."

"Perhaps Mademoiselle will sing a song for everyone," Marie-Grace suggested.

"What a good idea!" said Cécile.

Marie-Grace began to picture what it would be like if Mademoiselle recovered. *There could be a wedding after all,* Marie-Grace thought. She still felt sun-baked and tired. But Cécile had given her a glimmer of hope.

CHAPTER
TWO
—

A DESPERATE MISSION

Waves of heat were shimmering off the sidewalk when Marie-Grace arrived home that afternoon. Her father's wooden sign hung in front of his office. The faded letters read:

> ### Dr. Thaddeus Gardner
> ### Physician

But the front door was locked. Papa was still out seeing patients.

A black slate hung next to the office door. People wrote names and addresses of fever victims on the slate, and Dr. Gardner visited the homes as soon as he could. Marie-Grace saw that the slate was crowded with messages. Next to one of the names someone had written in large letters, PLEASE COME SOON!

Marie-Grace's heart fell. The full slate meant that Papa would not be home for a long time. Marie-Grace knew that the work her father was doing was important. But she missed him, and she wished she could talk to him about Mademoiselle Océane.

These days, Marie-Grace was often lonely. In the past, her family's housekeeper, Mrs. Curtis, had always been there when Marie-Grace had returned home. But now Mrs. Curtis was gone. Unlike Marie-Grace and her father—who had both survived yellow fever several years ago—Mrs. Curtis had never had the disease, and she had worried about getting it. When a neighbor's cook died of yellow fever, Mrs. Curtis had decided it was too dangerous to stay in New Orleans.

"Every day I see more and more coffins going to the graveyards," the housekeeper had told Marie-Grace and her father. "Half the people who've gotten sick have died from 'Yellow Jack.' I'm not going to be one of them!" Mrs. Curtis could not be convinced to stay another day. She had packed up her trunks and, with a tearful farewell, boarded a ship to Boston.

Now Marie-Grace had only Argos to keep her
company. When she stepped
through the gate behind her
father's office, the big dog was
waiting for her. Argos whined
eagerly, his tail thumping against
the courtyard wall.

"I'm glad to see you, too," Marie-Grace told him,
scratching behind his ears. The dog's water bowl
was almost empty, so Marie-Grace filled it from the
rain barrel. While Argos lapped up a long drink, she
splashed some cool water on her face. Then together
they climbed the stairs to the family's living quarters.

Marie-Grace found Mrs. Lambert, her neighbor,
sweeping the floor in the parlor. Dr. Gardner had
not yet found a live-in housekeeper to replace Mrs.
Curtis, so he had hired Mrs. Lambert to come in
each day to clean and cook. She was a large, cheerful
woman with a family of five children, and she had
helped the Gardners care for Philip before he was
taken to the orphanage.

Two weeks ago, Mrs. Lambert's son, Raoul, had
fallen ill with yellow fever. Dr. Gardner had done

everything he could to care for the child, and now the little boy was recovering. Mrs. Lambert, however, looked more tired than usual. She greeted Marie-Grace with a weary smile. "I'm glad to see you back," she said. "I have to be going soon, but I made a pot of *jambalaya* for you and your father."

The spicy smell of sausages and rice wafted in from the dining room, but Marie-Grace was still too worried to be hungry. "Thank you, Mrs. Lambert," she said. "I'll wait until Papa comes home so that we can eat together." *Maybe he'll have good news about Mademoiselle Océane,* she told herself.

Marie-Grace sat down at the piano and plunked the middle C note. Then she picked up the sheet music for *Amazing Grace.* Mademoiselle Océane had given it to her at their last lesson several weeks ago. Marie-Grace remembered how, when she first saw the music, she was surprised to see part of her own name in the title. "Is that why you chose it for me?" she'd asked.

"No, *chérie,*" Mademoiselle had said with a smile. "The song is about God's grace, not Marie-Grace."

Marie-Grace had blushed, but Mademoiselle had said that when she was younger, she had made a similar mistake. "I thought that a song about the ocean—*l'océan*—was about me, but of course it wasn't at all. I chose this song for you because it's very pretty, and it is perfect for your voice. I think you will like it."

Marie-Grace did like the hymn, but there was a long high note at the end of the first stanza that was hard for her. Mademoiselle had been teaching her to breathe so that she could sing the note properly. "You have a strong voice, Marie-Grace," Mademoiselle had encouraged her. "But you must learn how to use it."

If only Mademoiselle could be here with me now, thought Marie-Grace with an ache of loneliness. But the music made Marie-Grace feel closer to her teacher. She decided that she would practice the hymn until she could sing it perfectly. She took a deep breath and began.

> *Amazing grace, how sweet the sound,*
> *That saved a wretch like me.*

Marie-Grace's voice went flat on the last note. She sighed and tried again. And again. She kept practicing until Mrs. Lambert appeared.

"Oh, that's lovely!" Mrs. Lambert exclaimed from the doorway.

Marie-Grace felt her face turn red. She was always embarrassed to sing in front of people, but she'd been so caught up in the music that she'd forgotten Mrs. Lambert was there. "Thank you," Marie-Grace said shyly. "I still can't sing the high note quite right."

"Well, I think it sounds very nice," Mrs. Lambert declared. "It does me good to hear music. Can you sing—" Before Mrs. Lambert could finish her request, there was the sound of heavy footsteps on the stairs outside. Argos ran to the door. *Papa must be back early,* Marie-Grace thought.

But a moment later, Uncle Luc burst into the room. His suit was wrinkled, and he looked as if he had not slept in days. Instead of his usual affectionate greeting, Uncle Luc said breathlessly, "Marie-Grace, where is your father?"

"Papa's out seeing patients," said Marie-Grace. She searched her uncle's face for some hopeful sign. "How is Mademoiselle Océane?"

"She is worse than before," said Uncle Luc, shaking his head. "I must find your father."

Marie-Grace felt her stomach twist with fear. She'd never seen her uncle look so worried. "I don't know when he'll be back," Marie-Grace said.

"Would you like to leave Dr. Gardner a message, Monsieur Rousseau?" asked Mrs. Lambert. "I'm sure he'll call on you as soon as he can."

"I need help now. I can't wait," Uncle Luc insisted. "Océane is so sick that her landlady has had her moved to the infirmary at the Globe Ballroom."

"Surely Mademoiselle will get good care in the sick ward, Monsieur," Mrs. Lambert said.

"The doctors and nurses do their best," Uncle Luc admitted. He began to pace back and forth. "But there are so many people there. It's impossible for the nurses to care for everyone at once. What if Océane wakes and she is all alone? What if she needs water and can't call out? What then?"

Marie-Grace bit her lip. It was terrible to think of Mademoiselle suffering.

"I would sit with Océane day and night if I could," Uncle Luc continued. "But the infirmary's foolish rules do not permit me. They say that only women and girls are allowed. The only men who may stay in the women's ward are doctors or close family. Since I am neither, they won't let me visit my Océane for more than a few minutes."

"Was Mademoiselle awake when you last saw her? Could she talk with you?" asked Marie-Grace.

"No—she sleeps almost all the time. When she wakes, she is confused from the fever and does not know where she is." Uncle Luc sighed. "She needs someone to watch over her. But it seems as if everyone is either sick or caring for someone who is."

Uncle Luc stopped pacing in mid-stride. "What about you, Mrs. Lambert?" he asked. "Could you come and watch over Océane for me?"

"Oh, Monsieur, I am very sorry," said Mrs. Lambert, crinkling her forehead. "I'd be happy to help you if I could—indeed I would. But Raoul is still not strong. I need to go home to him and the other children as soon as I can."

Mrs. Lambert put her fingers to her lips for a moment, and then she brightened. "I know a very good nurse! Madame Jeannette—she's a free woman of color. She took care of a friend of mine, and the recovery was like a miracle! If she can't help you, perhaps she'll know someone who can."

"*Merci*, Mrs. Lambert. Thank you!" exclaimed

21

Uncle Luc. "I will stop at the infirmary for just a moment to see if Océane has awakened yet, and then I will find Madame Jeannette. Would you give me her address, please?"

As Mrs. Lambert wrote the address on a scrap of paper, Marie-Grace had an idea. She remembered her father saying that good nursing was even more important than medicine in the fight against yellow fever. "We doctors do all we can," he'd told her. "But a good nurse makes all the difference."

Maybe I could make the difference for Mademoiselle, she thought. She turned to her uncle. "May I come with you to the infirmary?"

He looked startled. "You, Marie-Grace?"

"Yes," she said with growing confidence. "I could stay with Mademoiselle Océane—that way she would not have to be alone. You said that they allow girls into the ward."

Uncle Luc shook his head doubtfully. "I'm not sure it would be a proper place for you, Marie-Grace. The people there are very sick, and it is"—he paused and searched for the right word—"*difficile.*"

"I won't mind if it's difficult," she told him. "I've helped Papa in sickrooms before."

22

"I think Marie-Grace would be a great comfort to Mademoiselle Océane," Mrs. Lambert chimed in.

Uncle Luc thought for a moment. "Very well," he said at last. "I'll take you with me, Marie-Grace. But we must leave now. We don't have a moment to lose."

Marie-Grace nodded. Then she thought about her father. "Would you let Papa know where I am going?" she asked Mrs. Lambert.

"If I see him," Mrs. Lambert said. "But I may be gone before he returns."

Marie-Grace had already grabbed her bonnet and was hurrying out the door with Uncle Luc. "You can leave him a message on the slate," she called over her shoulder to Mrs. Lambert.

Uncle Luc helped Marie-Grace into a hired coach. "Driver, hurry!" Uncle Luc ordered. The driver cracked his whip, and they set off over the granite-paved streets.

CHAPTER
THREE
—

FEVER AND ICE

 As the carriage rattled through the streets, Marie-Grace stared out the window. Everywhere she looked, she saw how the beautiful city was suffering from the epidemic. Dark fabric called mourning crepe hung from many houses, marking that someone who lived there had died. Shops were boarded shut, and several had large signs that read, "Closed until further notice."

On one corner, a barrel of burning tar sent clouds of smoke over the nearly empty streets. Marie-Grace held her handkerchief to her face. She knew that the smoke was supposed to help purify the air and protect the city from yellow fever. But the gray haze stung her throat and brought tears to her eyes.

The cathedral's bell rang out as they passed Jackson Square. Marie-Grace counted the chimes. It was five o'clock.

"Please hurry!" Uncle Luc called out to the driver. The carriage did not slow down until it pulled up in front of the Globe Ballroom. As soon as they lurched to a stop, Uncle Luc jumped out.

Marie-Grace followed him up the steps of the wide veranda. "It's as big as a hotel," she said, gazing at the building's impressive white columns.

"It was built for balls and parties," said Uncle Luc as he led the way through a set of double doors. "So many people are sick that several large buildings like this have been turned into temporary hospitals."

The lobby was crowded with people. "Wait here," Uncle Luc directed. "I'll only be a moment." Then he hurried up a wide circular staircase.

Marie-Grace tried to stay out of the way as doctors bustled past. People stood clustered together, talking loudly. A well-dressed woman was folding blankets with a nurse, and two men were carrying another man on a stretcher.

A throng of people were gathered on the far side

of the lobby. Marie-Grace craned her neck to see what was happening. Standing on her tiptoes, she saw a room with well-stocked shelves. Two weary-looking

 men were handing out supplies, taking donations, and answering questions all at once.

As the crowd pressed forward, no one seemed to take much notice of Marie-Grace. Then a voice behind her said, "Excuse me!" It sounded more like an order than a request. "I need to deliver these."

Marie-Grace turned around and saw a girl with an armful of blankets. "I'm sorry," Marie-Grace said as she moved aside. Then suddenly she realized that she knew this girl. "Lavinia?" she stammered in surprise. Lavinia Halsworth was the last person Marie-Grace would have expected to see at the infirmary.

Lavinia lowered the pile of blankets. She seemed just as surprised to see Marie-Grace. "What are *you* doing here?" Lavinia asked.

Marie-Grace swallowed hard. Lavinia was one of the wealthiest and most popular girls at school. Her bossy, know-it-all manner always made Marie-Grace uncomfortable. "I'm waiting to see a friend," Marie-Grace explained. "She's very sick."

"Well, I'm here with my mother," said Lavinia. She gestured toward the well-dressed woman on the other side of the lobby. "We're *helping*," Lavinia added. "Did you know that my sister got yellow fever?"

Marie-Grace shook her head. "I didn't know."

"She was *so* sick that everybody thought she was going to die," continued Lavinia. She scrunched up her face at the memory. "It was terrible. My father even ordered a coffin for her. Then my mother made a promise at church. She said that if my sister recovered, we'd help at the hospitals every day until the epidemic is over."

Lavinia nodded at the blankets in her arms. "Ever since my sister got better, we've been bringing supplies. Yesterday we brought food. Today it's blankets—and we're having ice delivered, too. It's very hard to find ice," Lavinia said proudly.

For a moment, Marie-Grace was speechless. She had never thought of Lavinia as someone who would be willing to help at an infirmary. "I'm glad your sister is better," Marie-Grace said finally. "And it's good of you to come here and help."

"I suppose," Lavinia agreed with a shrug. "At least we don't have to go up there." She gestured toward the circular staircase and made another face. "That's where all the sick people are."

Like Mademoiselle Océane, thought Marie-Grace.

Mrs. Halsworth beckoned to Lavinia. "I have to go," said Lavinia with an air of importance. "Perhaps I'll see you at school—whenever it starts. Have you heard that the schools won't open until the epidemic is over? Can you imagine that?"

Yes, I can, thought Marie-Grace. She started to tell Lavinia that the nuns who usually taught their classes were now busy helping at Holy Trinity Orphanage. But Lavinia didn't wait for a reply. Instead, with her usual bossy manner, she pushed her way through the crowd, saying, "Excuse me! Pardon me!"

A few minutes later, Uncle Luc returned, looking even paler than before. "I spoke with Nurse Emmeline, who's in charge of the women's ward. I arranged for you to sit with Océane until I get back."

"How is Mademoiselle Océane?"

"The same," he reported grimly. "Nurse Emmeline said she has not opened her eyes since she arrived."

Marie-Grace followed her uncle up the staircase. At the top of the landing, wide doors opened into what had once been a ballroom. The room had gold-painted ceilings and magnificent crystal chandeliers. But it was not the chandeliers that made Marie-Grace stare—it was the rows and rows of cots lined up inside the room.

"Gracious sakes!" she gasped.

Marie-Grace had heard Papa talk about the huge numbers of people who'd become sick with yellow fever during the last few months, but now she saw them for herself. She guessed that there had to be almost a hundred patients in this room alone, and there were other infirmaries set up around the city, too.

A round-faced woman in a white pinafore was sitting at a desk just outside the ballroom. There were dark circles under her eyes, and she frowned when Uncle Luc introduced Marie-Grace. "Monsieur Rousseau, you did not tell me that your niece was so young. How can she possibly be of help to Mademoiselle Océane?"

If Nurse Emmeline thinks I'm too young, I may never get the chance to see Mademoiselle, Marie-Grace worried. She stood as tall as she could. "I've helped in sickrooms before, ma'am," she volunteered.

Nurse Emmeline pursed her lips disapprovingly. "There was a young lady here today who fainted when she saw a little blood. You won't do that, will you?"

"No, ma'am," Marie-Grace assured her. "My father is Dr. Thaddeus Gardner. I've helped him lots of times, and I've never fainted at the sight of blood."

The nurse looked at her with new interest. "You're Dr. Gardner's daughter? Well, your father's one of the best doctors I know—he's a true hero."

Marie-Grace felt her face flush. Papa often talked about the brave nuns who risked their lives to nurse the sick. He also said that the Howard Association members were heroes. They were volunteers who worked day and night to help yellow fever victims. *Papa's never said anything about being a hero himself,* she thought.

Nurse Emmeline stood up and nodded to Marie-Grace. "Come with me."

"I'll be back as soon as I can," said Uncle Luc, and he disappeared down the stairs.

Marie-Grace took a deep breath. Then she

followed the nurse into the sea of cots.

Once, the ballroom had been an open space for dancing. Now it was divided in half by a heavy canvas curtain—male patients on one side, female on the other. Doctors and nurses hurried along the narrow paths between the cots, caring for as many people as possible.

Some patients had family members or friends sitting with them. Others were alone, and they banged on their bedside tables or called to passing nurses for help. Attendants were busy cleaning and mopping the floors, but the crowded room still had the stale smell of sickness.

Nurse Emmeline led the way to a corner of the ballroom near a balcony. Marie-Grace was shocked when she first saw Mademoiselle Océane lying motionless on the cot. She'd known that Mademoiselle was very ill, but she hadn't expected her eyes to be so sunken and her skin to be so yellow. Mademoiselle didn't even stir when Marie-Grace touched her shoulder and said hello.

"Is she going to be all right?" Marie-Grace whispered to the nurse.

"I don't know," said Nurse Emmeline. "We've

been hoping that her fever would break. But so far . . ." The nurse shook her head. "All we can do is give her our best care." She pointed to a small stool next to the cot. "You can sit down if you like."

Marie-Grace's legs felt a bit wobbly, but she didn't want the nurse to think that she might faint. "Thank you," she said as firmly as she could. "I'm fine standing for now."

Nurse Emmeline nodded approvingly. "If you need anything, ask at the desk—if anyone's there."

Another patient called for help, and Nurse Emmeline bustled away, leaving Marie-Grace standing alone by the cot. The doors to the balcony were open, but the sticky, warm air barely moved. A mosquito landed on Mademoiselle's forehead, and Marie-Grace flicked it away. *Papa says a good nurse makes her patient as comfortable as possible,* she told herself. *That's what I'll do.*

Marie-Grace peeled off her bonnet and set to work. She found a basin of water and a clean cloth and gently wiped Mademoiselle's face. Next she straightened the sheets and blankets on the cot and fluffed the pillow. Finally, she carefully brushed Mademoiselle's auburn hair.

As she worked, Marie-Grace talked, hoping that Mademoiselle could hear her. "Cécile and I thought you might like magnolias for your wedding," she said. She tried to sound as cheerful as she could. "But I wonder if roses would be better."

There was no response. But Marie-Grace kept talking. She chattered about Cécile, the little children at the orphanage, and Argos's latest adventures—all the things she would have told Mademoiselle if they had been sharing tea after lessons. When she finished brushing Mademoiselle Océane's hair, she braided it loosely and fastened it back with the silver comb that Mademoiselle always wore.

The comb was engraved with musical symbols. Looking at it, Marie-Grace remembered how Cécile had said that Armand was comforted by music when he was sick. "I've been practicing 'Amazing Grace,'" she told Mademoiselle. "I'm still having a bit of trouble, but I'm working on it. I'll sing it for you."

She sat down on the stool and began to quietly sing the hymn. As she sang, she reached for Mademoiselle's hand. It felt limp and lifeless, and

Mademoiselle did not move at all. Marie-Grace stopped singing. For one terrible moment, she was so frightened that she could barely breathe. She gripped Mademoiselle's hand. *Please don't die!* she pleaded silently. *Please!*

Suddenly, Mademoiselle Océane's eyes opened a slit. "Marie-Grace?" she murmured.

Marie-Grace felt a wave of relief. "Yes, it's me, Marie-Grace. I'm here, and Uncle Luc will be back soon, too. Would you like something? Water? Ice?" The words came tumbling out in a rush.

For a long moment, Mademoiselle Océane did not answer. She closed her eyes again as if the effort to keep them open was too painful. "Ice," she finally whispered.

"I'll get you some," Marie-Grace promised. "I'll be right back!" She hurried out to the hall, but Nurse Emmeline was not at the desk. Instead, a thin woman wearing a stained apron was sitting there. She shook her head when Marie-Grace asked for ice. "We've been out of ice since early this morning."

Marie-Grace remembered Lavinia. "There was supposed to be a delivery this afternoon."

"I don't know anything about that." The woman

shrugged. "You could ask downstairs."

Marie-Grace raced down the staircase. The lobby was even busier than it had been before. Dozens of people were standing in the middle of the hallway, all talking loudly in German. Marie-Grace did not know what they were saying. All she knew was that they were blocking her way to the ice she needed for Mademoiselle.

"Excuse me," she said politely, but no one paid attention. They just continued talking.

Why won't they move? Marie-Grace wondered. She felt her face burning. *Lavinia didn't let anyone stop her. And I'll bet Cécile wouldn't either.*

"Pardon me!" she said, louder this time. She tried to squeeze past, but two tall, bearded men were standing directly in her way. They didn't even notice that she was there.

I have to do something, Marie-Grace thought desperately. *Mademoiselle needs me.* Standing tall, she said in her loudest voice, "EXCUSE ME! I MUST GET THROUGH."

The two men looked surprised, but they stepped back enough to let her pass by. Marie-Grace raced to the supply room at the other end of the hall. "I need ice for a patient," Marie-Grace told the tired-looking man inside the cloakroom. "You have some, don't you?"

The man nodded. "Aye, a delivery just came," he said with an Irish accent. "No one's had time to take it up, but I'm sure I can give you some."

He reached into a zinc-lined box, scooped up a cup full of chipped ice, and handed it to Marie-Grace. She felt a thrill of triumph as she made her way back through the crowd. She could hardly wait to give Mademoiselle the cooling ice. Holding tight to the cup, she raced up the stairs to the ballroom.

SENT AWAY

Inside the ballroom, Marie-Grace propped pillows under Mademoiselle's head. Then she offered her a tiny spoonful of the ice chips. Mademoiselle smiled weakly at her first taste. "Merci," she whispered. "Thank you."

Marie-Grace had seen her father give ice to yellow fever patients. Now she offered the ice chips in the same way. She spooned them out slowly and watched to be sure that Mademoiselle did not choke.

Almost half the ice was gone when Uncle Luc appeared with Madame Jeannette.

"Océane! You're awake!" Uncle Luc cried, rushing to her side.

37

Marie-Grace offered Mademoiselle Océane a tiny spoonful of the ice chips.

"She asked for ice," Marie-Grace reported.

Madame Jeannette nodded. "That's a good sign," she said, putting her hand on Mademoiselle Océane's forehead. The dark-skinned nurse was tall, and her voice had an air of authority.

Mademoiselle Océane reached out her hand to Uncle Luc and whispered something to him. "Océane says you took good care of her, Marie-Grace," Uncle Luc said. A smile spread across his tired face. "And she says she's feeling better!"

Relief swept over Marie-Grace like a cooling breeze. *Wait until I tell Cécile,* she thought happily.

She was about to fetch a basin of fresh water when she heard a man's voice booming in the distance. "I'm looking for my daughter, Marie-Grace Gardner. Is she here?"

Surprised, Marie-Grace turned and saw her father standing in the doorway of the ballroom. She waved so that he could find her in the crowded room.

As soon as he caught sight of Marie-Grace, Dr. Gardner rushed toward her. Holding tight to his black medical bag, he ran along the narrow paths between the cots, brushing aside another doctor who was in his way. His face looked gray-white.

What's wrong? Marie-Grace wondered. She had never seen her father look so upset. *Is he angry that I'm here?* But when he reached her, her father did not say anything. Instead, he dropped his bag and picked her up in his arms. He hugged her tight, and his face felt damp and stubbly against her cheek.

"Thank heavens I found you!" he said when he put her down. Then he stepped back and studied her face. "What happened?" he asked urgently. "Tell me your symptoms."

Marie-Grace was puzzled. "I don't have any symptoms, Papa. I feel fine."

The furrows on her father's face deepened. "Then why are you here?"

"I came to help Mademoiselle," Marie-Grace explained. "You always say it's important for patients to have good nurses."

For a moment her father just stared at her. Then he sighed. Suddenly he looked very tired. "When I got home tonight, no one was there," he said slowly. "But there was a message on the slate that said, 'Marie-Grace at infirmary.'" He put his hand on her shoulder. "I was certain that you were hurt or sick. I've been all over the city looking for you."

Marie-Grace's hand flew to her mouth. "I'm sorry!" she said. "I asked Mrs. Lambert to leave a message on the slate. I didn't realize—"

"It was completely my fault, Thaddeus," Uncle Luc interrupted. "I hope you can forgive me—I never should have brought Marie-Grace here without your permission." He turned to Marie-Grace. "But I am very grateful for your help, Ti-Marie. You have been such a comfort to Océane. I can't thank you enough."

Papa rubbed his eyes wearily. "I suppose it was just a misunderstanding," he said finally. "In times like these, it's not surprising that such things could happen." Papa's face resumed its professional seriousness. "Now, let me see how the patient is doing."

Dr. Gardner looked into Mademoiselle's eyes and took her pulse. He spoke with the nurse for a few minutes, and then he turned back to Mademoiselle Océane. "You will be in good hands here with Madame Jeannette," he assured her. "Rest now, and I will call on you tomorrow."

Mademoiselle Océane reached for Marie-Grace. "Thank you, chérie," she said in a hoarse whisper.

"I hope you'll feel even better tomorrow," said

Marie-Grace, giving Océane's hand a squeeze.

While Uncle Luc stayed behind to talk with the nurse, Marie-Grace followed her father out through the maze of cots. She was surprised by the number of people who knew Papa. Two doctors stopped him to ask for his opinion on their cases. A Howard volunteer had questions for Papa, too. When they finally reached the hall, Nurse Emmeline was at her desk. "Dr. Gardner," she called. "May I speak to you?"

Marie-Grace watched from a distance as her father talked with the nurse. He seemed to agree with what she was saying, but his stern expression did not soften. A moment later he returned.

"Come, Marie-Grace," he said. "It's time for us to go home."

Outside, the sun had set, and not even a glimmer of light remained in the western sky. The evening air was hot and humid. Marie-Grace swatted at a mosquito that hovered around her head. Suddenly she was exhausted and almost faint with hunger.

"What time is it?" she asked.

Her father pulled out his pocket watch. "It's nearly nine-thirty."

I've been here for more than four hours! Marie-Grace realized. She had been so busy that it seemed as though less than an hour had passed since she'd left home. *No wonder Papa was worried.*

She and her father climbed into a hired carriage. As soon as they were settled on the seats, Marie-Grace told her father about everything that had happened. Finally, she told him about the worst moment. "When Mademoiselle was sleeping, she hardly moved at all, even when I held her hand. I was so afraid. I . . . I thought she might be dead."

"Even people with years of experience can sometimes be fooled," he assured her. "But doctors and nurses check a patient's breathing and heartbeat. Try to feel your own heart beating."

It took Marie-Grace a moment to find the right spot on her chest. When she finally felt the reassuring heartbeat, she smiled. *I'll remember that,* she thought. She relaxed against the carriage cushion and tried to fight off sleep. It was comforting to talk to her father. He understood what it had been like in the infirmary. Now she could understand what it was like for him to spend long nights caring for patients.

"Nurse Emmeline told me what good work you did tonight, Marie-Grace," Papa said quietly. "She said that many people twice your age would not have done nearly so well." He paused and then added, "I'm proud of you."

It was dark inside the carriage, but Marie-Grace beamed with happiness. From her father, those were words of highest praise. As the carriage wheels rattled down the road, Marie-Grace heard them repeating, "I'm-proud-of-you, I'm-proud-of-you, I'm-proud-of-you."

Her father cleared his throat. "But I've made a decision," he said. "Tomorrow, I'm sending you to Belle Chênière."

Suddenly, Marie-Grace was wide awake. Belle Chênière was the small town not far from New Orleans where her mother had grown up. Marie-Grace looked forward to visiting her relatives there someday—but not now. Not when Mademoiselle and so many others were sick here in New Orleans.

"We can't go!" she protested. "You said you'd call on Mademoiselle Océane tomorrow."

"*I'm* staying here," her father said firmly. "Only

you are going, Marie-Grace. Now that you've been inside the infirmary, you know how serious this epidemic is. It's worse than any that's ever hit New Orleans. You'll be safer in Belle Chênière."

Marie-Grace was stunned by her father's decision. "Why do I have to leave, Papa? I won't catch yellow fever. I've already had it, just as you have. I want to stay here with you."

For a long moment, her father was silent. Then he said quietly, "When I came home and saw the message that you were at the infirmary, I was more afraid than I've ever been in my life. I realized that I've been away too much caring for others—and I've left you alone to care for yourself."

"But Papa—" Marie-Grace began.

"No," her father interrupted. "I don't want you to be alone anymore. When the epidemic is over, we'll find another housekeeper. Until then, you will stay with your Great-Aunt Lisette. I'm taking you to the levee tomorrow. You'll go by steamboat to Belle Chênière."

Marie-Grace knew by her father's tone that it was useless to argue. She sat hunched in the corner of the carriage, her arms crossed over her chest. Now she could feel her heart easily—it was pounding like a hammer in her chest.

This is my home, she thought as the carriage rumbled through the winding streets. *Why is Papa sending me away?*

Outside the carriage, the creaking wheels repeated, "Sending-me-away, sending-me-away, sending-me-away."

ALL ABOARD

Marie-Grace's battered old trunk sat in the middle of her room. On her bed was a pile of neatly folded clothes. Marie-Grace fought back tears as she opened the trunk and slowly began to pack. She and Papa had moved many times before. But ever since they had arrived back in New Orleans, she'd hoped that they would stay here forever.

Now I'm moving again, she thought as her petticoat landed at the bottom of the trunk. *But Papa's not coming with me.*

She'd never been away from her father for more than a day. Even if Papa took care of patients until late at night, he always came home as soon as he could. Now Marie-Grace knew that she might not see him for weeks—or even months.

I'll miss Cécile, she told herself as she packed her gray dress. It was the dress that she had worn the day she met Cécile. *She's my first true friend,* Marie-Grace thought. *And now we won't be able to help at Holy Trinity together.*

Marie-Grace reached for the beautiful lace-trimmed green jacket that Mademoiselle Océane had given her. *And what about Mademoiselle?* she thought. *She's still sick, and it will take so long to get news of her in Belle Chênière!* Marie-Grace hugged the jacket close to her heart before placing it carefully in the trunk.

Finally, Marie-Grace took her most prized possession, the framed portrait of her mother, from her bedside table. She tucked it in among the clothes so that it would be safe. Then, with a sigh, she closed the trunk.

She sat down beside Argos, who was lying next to her bed. "I don't want to leave you," she told the big dog. "But Papa said he'll take good care of you while I'm gone, and Mrs. Lambert will make sure you have food and water."

Argos nuzzled her, and she buried her face in his fur. "I'll be back as soon as I can, I promise," she whispered to the dog.

"Marie-Grace, it's time to go!" Papa called from his office.

Marie-Grace slowly stood up. She and Argos walked together down the stairs and across the courtyard. Argos stayed close by her side, as if he understood that she was going away.

Papa was busy writing when Marie-Grace and Argos entered his office. "Are you ready, Grace?" he asked as he signed a prescription.

Marie-Grace nodded reluctantly. Then she burst out, "Please don't make me go, Papa! I want to stay here and help at the orphanage, and I want to help Mademoiselle Océane, too. Other girls are staying. Cécile helps at the orphanage, and even Lavinia goes to the infirmary."

Her father looked up from his stack of papers. There were dark shadows under his eyes. "Those girls have parents who can watch over them," he explained. "I must be gone most of the time."

"But Papa—" Marie-Grace began.

Her father shook his head. "You are sailing today,

49

Marie-Grace. The arrangements have been made."

Marie-Grace knew that a daughter must respect her father's wishes. But she had one more request. "Could I please visit Holy Trinity before I go? Cécile should be there, and I want to say good-bye to her."

Her father pushed his paperwork aside. "Very well. If we leave now, we'll have time for a short visit on our way to the levee," he said. "Let's get your trunk."

As soon as Marie-Grace arrived at the orphanage, Pierre ran up to her. He pointed hopefully toward the swings.

Marie-Grace shook her head. "I can't push you on the swings today," she said sadly. The little boy's shoulders slumped with disappointment, and Marie-Grace couldn't bear to leave him by himself. "Come with me," she said, holding out her hand. She led Pierre to a group of children playing in the shade and helped him join their game. Then she headed across the courtyard to Cécile.

Her friend was wearing a pink bonnet and

skipping rope with several little girls. "Tinker, tailor, soldier, sailor ..." Cécile chanted as her bonnet strings bobbed up and down. When Cécile saw Marie-Grace, she broke off her chant and ran over. "What's wrong? You look so sad. Do you have news about Mademoiselle Océane?"

"I have good news," Marie-Grace answered. She told Cécile all about her visit to the infirmary.

"That *is* good news!" Cécile's face lit up with a bright smile. "When Armand started asking for ice, we knew he was getting better!"

"I have bad news, too," Marie-Grace admitted, and she told Cécile about Papa's decision.

"Oh no! You *can't* go away!" Cécile exclaimed. "Sister Beatrice needs us both to help as much as we can. The children ask for you if you're not here. And *I* will miss you."

Marie-Grace felt tears welling up in her eyes. "I *want* to stay here, but Papa says I have to go."

"There must be some way to make him change his mind," said Cécile, frowning.

Marie-Grace's eyebrows shot up. "Do you have any ideas?"

"Oh, I wish I did," said Cécile sympathetically.

She kicked a pebble across the courtyard.

Just then, Katy ran up and tugged on Marie-Grace's skirt with dusty hands. "Marie-the-Great, come play!"

Marie-Grace saw her father walking toward her, and she knew it was time to leave. She leaned over and gave Katy a hug. "I can't play right now, Katy. I have to go away for a while. But I'll come back as soon as I can."

Katy held tight to Marie-Grace's skirt. "Don't go away! Stay here with me."

"I can't," Marie-Grace said, and she gently tried to loosen Katy's hands.

"Why not?" Katy demanded. "Sister Beatrice would let you."

"What if . . ." Cécile began. But before she could say anything more, Marie-Grace's father joined them.

"We must leave, Grace," Dr. Gardner announced.

Katy began to sob. "No!" she cried. She shook her head so hard that her braids flew back and forth.

"Come, Katy, let's go see Sister Beatrice," Cécile said. She scooped up the crying child and carried her into the orphanage.

As she watched Cécile and Katy disappear into

the building, Marie-Grace felt all her hope vanish with them. *I didn't even say good-bye,* she realized.

"May I go see Sister Beatrice, too?" she asked her father. "Just for a moment?"

Papa checked his pocket watch. "No, Grace. I know it's hard to leave, but there isn't time for more farewells. We can't be late for the sailing."

A short, piercing whistle signaled that the *Victoria* was about to leave. Marie-Grace stood on the deck of the steamboat and waved to her father with her handkerchief. He was standing on the dock with his medical bag at his feet. Despite the pounding sun, he had taken off his hat and was waving farewell to her with it.

"Good-bye, Papa!" Marie-Grace called. She felt a lump in her throat. Her father looked so alone on the dock. *Who will be there to help him when I'm gone?* she wondered.

Behind her father, the white spires of St. Louis Cathedral soared into the blue sky. Ten months ago, on her first day back in New Orleans, Uncle Luc had taken her on a carriage ride through the city. When they had passed the cathedral, Marie-Grace had thought it was a castle in a fairy tale. It was the most beautiful building she had ever seen.

Since that day, Marie-Grace had walked past the cathedral hundreds of times. She had gone inside to worship, and she had prayed for Mademoiselle's recovery there too.

Now as she looked at the beautiful cathedral, it reminded her of everything she loved about New Orleans. She thought about Papa and Argos, about Uncle Luc and Mademoiselle Océane, about Cécile, and about Sister Beatrice and all the orphans at Holy Trinity.

I don't want to leave, Marie-Grace thought. *I belong here.* Tears trickled down her cheeks, and she turned away so that Papa wouldn't see her crying. She scrubbed her face with her handkerchief. Then she turned back to the levee so that she could wave to Papa again.

But her father was no longer alone. A nun in long black robes was with him, along with a girl in a pink bonnet. It was Sister Beatrice and Cécile! Hope flashed through Marie-Grace like lightning.

The steamboat's whistle blew two piercing blasts, and the last passengers scrambled aboard with their satchels and trunks. As the crew members were about to pull up the gangplank, Marie-Grace's father broke away from the others and hurried up the ramp. She ran to meet him.

"Sister Beatrice came here to tell me what a great help you are with the orphans," said her father, slightly out of breath. "She's offered to let you stay at Holy Trinity for now."

Marie-Grace thought of Katy's words—"Sister Beatrice would let you stay." *Cécile must have talked to Sister Beatrice!* thought Marie-Grace excitedly.

Her father continued, "You wouldn't be alone when I'm gone, and you could keep helping the nuns with the children. Would you like to do that?"

"Oh, yes, Papa!" Marie-Grace exclaimed.

Papa held her at arm's length. "Are you sure, Marie-Grace?" he asked, his forehead creased with worry lines. "I want you to think carefully before you choose. There are going to be hard times ahead. Life would be much easier for you in Belle Chênière."

"You could keep helping the nuns with the children.
Would you like to do that?" Papa asked.

56

The steamboat whistle shrieked again—once, twice, three times. The *Victoria* was about to sail. Marie-Grace did not hesitate. "I'm not afraid, Papa," she said, looking at him steadily. "I want to stay here and help, just like you."

A smile broke out across her father's face. He reached for her hand. "Well, then," he said, "let's go get your trunk."

Sister Beatrice and Cécile were waiting on the levee when Marie-Grace and her father returned together. Cécile was grinning triumphantly.

"I was afraid we'd be too late," she whispered to Marie-Grace as they walked back to the orphanage together. "Sister Beatrice doesn't walk very fast."

"You were just in time," Marie-Grace whispered back. "Thank you. Papa says I can stay."

"Good!" said Cécile. "Because we have lots of work to do." She grinned again. "Besides, Katy is waiting for you!"

Marie-Grace soon discovered that her father was right—there were hard times ahead. Holy Trinity was bursting with children, and Marie-Grace served meals, rocked babies, read stories, and cleaned up messes. Cécile came to help as often as she could, too. Sometimes the girls sang together while they worked or when they played with the children. But the chores still seemed endless.

A few days after Marie-Grace moved in, several sick children arrived at the orphanage and needed extra care. "Thank heavens you're here, Marie-Grace," Sister Beatrice said after the two of them had spent an especially hard afternoon with a sick baby. "I don't know what we would do without you."

Sister Beatrice's kind words warmed Marie-Grace's heart, and she was glad she was at the orphanage. But she missed Papa terribly. She looked forward to his daily visits, and she always asked him about Mademoiselle Océane.

"Mademoiselle is slowly getting better," he told her every day. "But we have to be patient."

At the end of the first week, Papa brought Argos to the orphanage. The big dog wagged his tail furiously when he saw Marie-Grace, and he jumped up and licked her face. "I missed you, too," said Marie-Grace, hugging him.

It was early afternoon, and most of the children were resting inside, so the courtyard was quiet. Papa and Marie-Grace sat on the grass under the shade of the magnolia tree. Argos sprawled close to Marie-Grace, and she scratched behind his ears while she told Papa the news at Holy Trinity. One little boy had gone to live with his grandmother, but a pair of orphaned sisters had arrived early that morning.

Then Papa shared his news. "Mademoiselle is finally well enough to leave the infirmary," he said.

"That's wonderful!" Marie-Grace exclaimed excitedly. "Can we go visit her, Papa? Please?"

He shook his head. "She's gone to the country to recover and won't be back for several weeks. I hope the epidemic will be over by then so you'll be able to come home, too."

Marie-Grace's heart sank. *How many weeks is several?* she wondered as sweat trickled down her back. She was hot and tired, and even one week seemed like forever. She leaned against Argos, and the big dog nuzzled her sympathetically.

Papa touched her shoulder. "Don't give up hope, Grace," he said gently. "Things will get better, I promise. We just have to keep working."

She looked up at her father. The shadows under his eyes were darker than ever, and deep lines were etched in his forehead. She realized that Papa was tired, too, but he was working as hard as he could. Marie-Grace thought of Sister Beatrice and the other nuns at Holy Trinity, the Howard volunteers, and all the nurses, doctors, and other people in New Orleans who were bravely fighting the epidemic.

She squared her shoulders with determination. *I'll keep fighting, too,* she decided.

In the weeks that followed, Marie-Grace's days passed in a blur of chores, crying babies, and small children clinging to her. Sometimes she was so tired that she fell asleep during evening prayers. But she refused to give up.

CHAPTER
SIX
—
JOY

As October began, the weather
cooled, and there were fewer new
cases of yellow fever. Many people
who had fled the city decided that it was safe to come
back. More and more ships began to dock along the
levee, and carriages full of families clattered through
the streets. The tempting smell of roasting coffee once
again filled the air, shops reopened, and customers
returned to the markets and cafés.

One bright afternoon, Marie-Grace was sitting in
the courtyard with Katy, showing her how to braid
long stalks of grass, when Sister Beatrice called to her.
"Marie-Grace, you have visitors!"

Marie-Grace stood up, expecting to see Papa

and Argos. Instead, she saw a dark-haired man walking arm-in-arm with a slender young woman. It took Marie-Grace a moment to recognize the woman. Then she raced across the dusty path—into Mademoiselle Océane's arms.

After a flurry of kisses and hugs, Marie-Grace learned that Mademoiselle Océane had arrived back in New Orleans just an hour earlier. "We came to see you right away," Mademoiselle said. "We want to share our good news."

"Good news?" echoed Marie-Grace. She looked from Uncle Luc to Mademoiselle Océane. Mademoiselle was thinner now, but her eyes were bright, and both she and Uncle Luc were glowing with happiness. *Could it be?* Marie-Grace wondered. She felt her heart racing.

"Yes!" Uncle Luc exclaimed. He looked fondly at Mademoiselle Océane. "We are to be married in three days, right here at the Holy Trinity chapel."

Marie-Grace clapped her hands. "Wait until I tell Cécile! We've both been hoping, but we didn't know it would be so soon!"

Mademoiselle will be my aunt! Marie-Grace thought happily. The sunshine seemed brighter than ever, and Marie-Grace suddenly remembered all the plans that she and Cécile had made. "Cécile said she could bring flowers to the wedding—her garden is full," she said, the words tumbling out in a rush. "And is there anything I could do?"

"You have already done so much for me, chérie," said Mademoiselle Océane, her blue eyes shining. "I will never forget your kindness when I was sick. It made such a difference to know that you were there with me." She paused and then added, "But there is one more favor I would like to ask of you."

"I'll be happy to do anything, Mademoiselle, anything at all!" Marie-Grace offered.

"I have often thought of the song you sang for me at the infirmary," Mademoiselle began hesitantly.

"We'd like you to sing it at the wedding, Ti-Marie," Uncle Luc finished.

"You want *me* to sing?" Marie-Grace asked with surprise. She felt her stomach flip-flop with nervousness. She loved singing in Mademoiselle's studio, and she often sang at Holy Trinity. But singing with little children was very different from singing for grown-ups. "Don't you want to sing the hymn yourself, Mademoiselle?"

"My voice is not yet strong," Mademoiselle explained. She smiled at Marie-Grace. "And I know you can sing the song beautifully."

Marie-Grace felt her stomach flip-flop again. But at that moment, she was too happy to be nervous. "I'll try," she promised.

⊛

The morning of the wedding was bright, with a hint of autumn coolness. In her tiny room at Holy Trinity, Marie-Grace dressed with special care. First she put on her best clothes—the taffeta skirt and beautiful green jacket that Mademoiselle Océane had given her. Then she put on her best silk shoes. It had been so long since she had worn them that they now pinched her toes a bit. Finally, she put on her bonnet and tied the ribbons in a bow. *I'm ready,* she thought with a thrill of anticipation—and nervousness.

Before she left the room, Marie-Grace made sure that everything was packed in her trunk. After the wedding, she was finally moving back to her own house for good!

Marie-Grace couldn't wait to be with Papa and

Argos again. But she felt a small pang as she closed the door and headed downstairs. She'd always wanted to be part of a large family, and during the last six weeks, she had come to feel like a big sister to all the children at Holy Trinity.

As soon as Marie-Grace appeared in the crowded courtyard, several children came running over to her. Marie-Grace's skirt rustled as she reached down and hugged each child.

"Oh, Marie-the-Great, you look so pretty!" exclaimed Katy.

"Thank you," said Marie-Grace.

Charlie crossed his arms over his chest. "Will you really come back to see us?" he asked.

"Yes, Charlie," Marie-Grace reassured him. She had explained this yesterday, but Charlie still looked worried. "I'll come every morning next week. Once school starts again, I'll come in the afternoons, as often as I can."

"*Avec* Argos?" asked Pierre, who loved to curl up with the big dog.

"I can't bring Argos with me *every* day," Marie-Grace told him. "But I'll bring him sometimes." She glanced up and saw Cécile heading into the chapel with baskets full of flowers. "Now I have to go get ready for the wedding."

"Wait!" called Katy. Her copper-brown braids were shining in the sun, and she was holding something behind her back. "I made this for you."

Katy opened her hands and showed Marie-Grace a bracelet of braided grass. The grass had dried and turned brown, but Katy was bursting with excitement as she presented it.

"What a pretty bracelet!" said Marie-Grace, holding it up for everyone to admire. She felt a lump in her throat as she thanked Katy and kissed her on the top of her head. "I'll see you all tomorrow, I promise."

Marie-Grace ran across the noisy courtyard and into the quiet chapel. The church was not very big, but the arched ceiling stretched so high that Marie-Grace had to crane her neck to see the top. The pews were made of polished wood, and tall windows illuminated everything in a glow of light.

So far, there were only a few other people in the chapel. Cécile was at the altar with baskets of canna lilies and hibiscus flowers. She turned when Marie-Grace entered.

"I'm glad you're here!" said
Cécile softly. "I brought all the
flowers from our garden. But we
don't have much time to arrange
them."

As Marie-Grace helped place
the colorful flowers in vases, she told her friend
her good news. "Papa's hired a housekeeper," she
whispered excitedly. "So after the wedding, I'm going
home!"

"That's wonderful," Cécile exclaimed. "But
what about the children here at Holy Trinity? They
will miss you terribly. What will Katy and Pierre do
without you?"

"I'll miss them all, too," Marie-Grace said,
thinking about the braided bracelet that Katy had
given her. "But I'm going to keep helping. Your
mother will still let you come too, won't she?"

"Yes, of course," Cécile whispered. "Maman
says that even though the worst of the epidemic is
over, there's still a lot to do. The city is just starting to
return to life again."

The girls were tucking the last flowers into
the vases when Sister Beatrice appeared. "It's almost

time to begin, girls," she said.

The girls picked up the empty baskets. When Marie-Grace turned around, she was surprised to see how full the chapel was. Cécile slipped into a pew near the front, and Marie-Grace slid in next to her.

"I'm so happy that you got to stay in New Orleans, Marie-Grace," Cécile whispered. "Just think, you would have missed the wedding if you had gone to Belle Chênière."

"I know," Marie-Grace whispered back. She thought of the moment on the steamboat when she'd felt as if she were leaving New Orleans forever. She smiled at Cécile. "I wouldn't want to be anywhere else in the world," she told her friend.

Uncle Luc walked in. He looked very handsome in a dark suit as he stood expectantly by the altar. Then the priest entered, and a nun began to play the organ. Everyone stood up and turned toward the back of the chapel.

"Oh!" gasped Marie-Grace.

Mademoiselle was wearing a simple ivory-colored dress trimmed in lace, and she carried a single white lily. She looked beautiful and radiantly happy. Papa was dressed in his best suit. He escorted

Mademoiselle Océane down the center aisle. When they reached the altar, Mademoiselle took Uncle Luc's hand.

Papa joined Marie-Grace. As they sat down, he whispered, "Here's your music in case you need it." He took three sheets of paper out of his jacket pocket, unfolded them, and set them on the pew next to Marie-Grace.

The song! In all the excitement, Marie-Grace had almost forgotten that she was going to sing. Now she felt the familiar flutter of anxiety in her stomach. *Don't think about it now,* she told herself. *Just think about the wedding.*

As the priest spoke in French, Marie-Grace smiled to herself. She understood every word. Less than a year ago, French had been hard for her. Now it was easy.

At last, the priest said, "I pronounce you man and wife."

Mademoiselle Océane lifted her veil, and she and Uncle Luc kissed. *Now she is truly my Aunt Océane,* Marie-Grace thought, and she sighed with happiness.

Marie-Grace felt a nudge in her ribs. "It's time for

the song," Cécile said in a low voice.

Uncle Luc and Aunt Océane stepped to one side of the altar, and Aunt Océane nodded to Marie-Grace. Cécile gave Marie-Grace's hand a quick squeeze of encouragement.

People rustled in their seats, and Marie-Grace knew that everyone was waiting for her. She stood up and made her way past her father to the center aisle. When she turned to face the crowd, she discovered that she'd left her music on the pew. Her mouth went dry. *I can't remember the words!* she thought in a panic.

Then she saw Papa looking at her through his wire-rim glasses. He was smiling proudly, and his eyes were filled with love. Suddenly, Marie-Grace realized that she didn't need the music. She knew it all by heart. She took a deep breath. Then she began to sing:

Amazing grace, how sweet the sound . . .

The beginning was always the hardest part for her. She worried that she'd sound as nervous as she felt and that her voice would crack on the high note

Suddenly, Marie-Grace realized that she didn't need the music.
She knew it all by heart.

71

she had practiced so many times. But as she sang, her voice gained strength.

By the time she reached the third verse, Marie-Grace had forgotten all her shyness. She looked around the chapel and saw her family and friends smiling up at her. Marie-Grace sang out loud and clear,

> *Through many dangers, toils, and snares*
> *I have already come.*
> *'Tis grace has brought me safe thus far*
> *and grace will lead me home.*

I am home, Marie-Grace thought, joy bubbling up inside her. *I'm finally home!*

LOOKING BACK

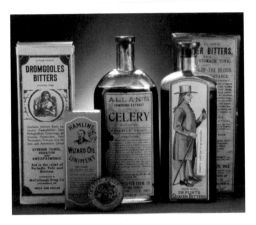

HEALTH AND MEDICINE
IN AMERICA IN
1853

Garbage collection was limited in most American cities throughout the 1800s. People threw their trash into the streets, and that's usually where it stayed.

When Marie-Grace was growing up, America was not a healthy place to live. People often consumed food and water that were not safe. There were no refrigerators to prevent harmful bacteria from growing, so food spoiled quickly. Drinking water usually came from the same rivers that were used as dumping grounds for garbage and human waste. Trash and horse droppings littered city streets.

Personal *hygiene*, or cleanliness to maintain health, was also different than it is today. In the early 1800s, people washed daily, but they seldom took baths. They thought that cleaning the

In Marie-Grace's time, people regularly washed their faces, hands, and feet in basins of water.

74

whole body at once would make them sick. By 1853, most people knew that baths weren't bad for them, but taking one wasn't easy. Since there was no indoor plumbing, water had to be carried into a home by hand, heated, and then poured into a tub. This was a lot of work, so most people bathed only a few times a month.

Disease spread quickly in these unclean conditions. But no one knew why. Even the best doctors and scientists didn't yet understand what germs were or that they caused disease. Doctors went from one patient to the next without washing their hands or their medical instruments. They didn't know that they were spreading germs and making people sick.

When people got sick, the treatment sometimes made them worse instead of better. Bleeding, for example, was believed to release the "bad blood" that contained disease. Doctors opened a patient's vein to drain some of the blood. Since the instruments were not *sterile*, or clean, patients could develop infections and get even sicker. Some patients lost so much blood that they fainted. Many doctors believed that bleeding was an effective cure. They used it to treat everything from a serious fever to a bruise from a fall.

Marie-Grace's father kept a jar of leeches in his office. Physicians like Dr. Gardner would place a leech on a person's skin and let the wormlike creature suck the blood out.

In 1853, most medicines simply were not effective at curing serious illnesses. Some were actually dangerous. Calomel (KAL-uh-mel), for example, was a popular medicine, but too much of it could be fatal. Patients were told to take calomel until they developed an excessive amount of saliva in their mouths. Doctors thought it was a sign that the treatment was working, but it really meant that the patient was being poisoned!

Many medicines didn't harm people, but they didn't help, either. In the 1800s, anything could be labeled as medicine. *Patent medicines* were the various tonics, syrups, tablets, and ointments that promised miracle cures for everything from stomachaches to pimples to baldness. One of the most popular cure-all patent medicines was Dr. Miles's Compound Extract of Tomato. It's still sold today, but it's called ketchup!

A traveling doctor selling homemade medicine

The ingredients in patent medicines were kept secret. They were usually made from herbs, and most of them contained a great deal of alcohol. Some medicines even included deadly substances such as turpentine and kerosene. Unlike today, the makers of these medicines did not have to prove that their tonics were effective or

Advertisements for patent medicines and the labels on the bottles promised fast relief for all sorts of ailments.

even safe. One store in Topeka, Kansas, displayed a sign that read, "We sell patent medicines but do not recommend them."

In the 1800s, almost all health care took place at home. Wives and mothers often consulted medical manuals and self-help books, or tried home remedies that they had learned from their own mothers. When people decided they needed a doctor, the doctor came to them. Physicians made house calls more often than they treated patients in offices or hospitals. Like Marie-Grace's father, most doctors did their best to cure people with the knowledge, tools, and medicines they had.

When sickness struck, families kept a constant watch over their loved ones—just as Marie-Grace did when Mademoiselle Océane

Doctors took boxes or bags of supplies when they went on house calls.

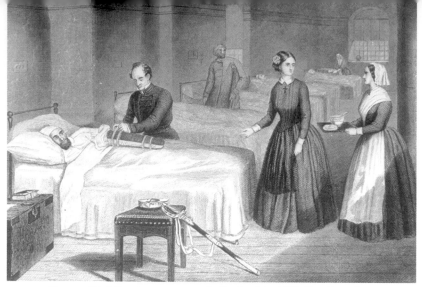

Florence Nightingale was a nurse in England in 1853. Her ideas about hygiene and sanitation greatly influenced American nursing.

fell ill. Friends and neighbors took turns staying throughout the night so that family members could rest. Such compassion was also extended to strangers. When a Boston merchant traveling through Worcester, Massachusetts, became seriously ill, a lawyer whom he had known for only a day took over his care. The lawyer spent more than a week nursing the sick stranger until he was well enough to go home.

During the yellow fever epidemic of 1853, women and girls in New Orleans really did volunteer at temporary infirmaries. They tended patients so that the nurses could get a few hours of sleep. Good nursing generally saved more lives than aggressive medical treatments. Patients who were kept cool and comfortable, bathed, and given liquids tended to recover more quickly than patients who were bled or given medicines. Yet as important as nursing was, women received very little formal training. They learned the job from their mothers or from other nurses. Nursing was thought of as something certain women were born to do, much like a religious calling. That idea may have come from the fact that nuns provided many nursing services throughout the 1800s.

The first nursing school opened in America in 1872. Around that time, people were beginning to understand the role that germs play in causing diseases. In the United States today, there are fewer diseases that are likely to become epidemics. Living conditions are much cleaner and safer than they were when Marie-Grace was growing up. Doctors and scientists have a better understanding of how the body works, and medicines are more effective at curing illness.

By the 1870s, vaccinations had been developed to keep people safe from deadly diseases like smallpox.

GLOSSARY OF FRENCH WORDS

avec *(ah-vek)*—with

chérie *(shay-ree)*—dear, darling

difficile *(dee-fee-seel)*—difficult

jambalaya *(zhum-buh-lah-yuh)*—a delicious stew of rice cooked with ham, sausage, chicken, shrimp, or oysters and seasoned with herbs

l'océan *(loh-say-ahn)*—the ocean

Madame *(mah-dahm)*—Mrs., ma'am

Mademoiselle *(mahd-mwah-zel)*—Miss

maman *(mah-mahn)*—mother, mama

merci *(mehr-see)*—thank you

Monsieur *(muh-syuh)*—Mr., sir

Prépare-toi. *(pray-par twah)*—Get ready.

tante *(tahnt)*—aunt

How to Pronounce French Names

Armand *(ar-mahn)*

Belle Chênière *(bel sheh-nyehr)*—a fictional village outside of New Orleans where Marie-Grace's relatives live. The name means "beautiful oak grove."

Cécile Rey *(say-seel ray)*

Emmeline *(em-uh-leen)*

Jeannette *(zhah-net)*

Lisette *(lee-zet)*

Luc Rousseau *(lewk roo-soh)*

Océane *(oh-say-ahn)*

Pierre *(pyehr)*

Raoul *(rah-ool)*

Ti-Marie *(tee-mah-ree)*—Marie-Grace's nickname. "Ti" is short for *petit,* or "little," so the nickname means "Little Marie."

GET THE WHOLE STORY

Two very different girls share a unique friendship and a remarkable story. Cécile's and Marie-Grace's books take turns describing the year that changes both their lives. Read all six!

Available at bookstores and at *americangirl.com*

BOOK 1: MEET MARIE-GRACE

When Marie-Grace arrives in New Orleans, she's not sure she fits in—until an unexpected invitation opens the door to friendship.

BOOK 2: MEET CÉCILE

Cécile plans a secret adventure at a glittering costume ball. But her daring plan won't work unless Marie-Grace is brave enough to take part, too!

BOOK 3: MARIE-GRACE AND THE ORPHANS

Marie-Grace discovers an abandoned baby. With Cécile's help, she finds a safe place for him. But when a fever threatens the city, she wonders if *anyone* will be safe.

BOOK 4: TROUBLES FOR CÉCILE

Yellow fever spreads through the city—and into Cécile's own home. Marie-Grace offers help, but it's up to Cécile to be strong when her family needs her most.

BOOK 5: MARIE-GRACE MAKES A DIFFERENCE

As the fever rages on, Marie-Grace and Cécile volunteer at a crowded orphanage. Then Marie-Grace discovers that it's not just the orphans who need help.

BOOK 6: CÉCILE'S GIFT

The epidemic is over, but it has changed Cécile—and New Orleans—forever. With Marie-Grace's encouragement, Cécile steps onstage to help her beloved city recover.

82

A SNEAK PEEK AT
THE NEXT BOOK IN THE SERIES

Cécile's
GIFT

The carriage turned a corner, and the *clip-clop* of the horses' hooves slowed. Cécile glanced out the window. They were passing a cemetery only a few blocks from Papa's stone yard. The street was clogged with wagons of every size and type, and almost all of them carried long wooden boxes, also of different sizes. As the carriage inched along, Cécile realized that the boxes were coffins . . . coffins for those who had died, like Ellen and Perrine's maman and papa.

Cécile wanted to look away, but she couldn't. For the first time, she understood why Papa had been so very busy lately. He was a stone mason. He carved fancy marble mantels and urns and even fountains . . . and when someone died, if the family could afford it, Papa carved an elegant stone marker and etched the person's name on it.

Monsieur Antoine turned into the winding drive of Papa's stone yard, clucking and coaxing his horses through the tall iron gates. When the carriage came to a stop, Cécile scrambled out first. The gravel of the driveway crunched underneath her boots, and she heard the *clink-clank* of tools ringing out of the wide shop doors.

Cécile watched Maman go into the workshop to kiss Papa on the cheek and greet the workers, but she didn't follow. She didn't want to go inside the workshop, where the tombstones were.

At the side of the drive, Tante Tay spread a tablecloth over two long planks laid across wooden barrels. Monsieur Antoine began to unload the heavy crocks and baskets of food. Cécile caught the scent of spicy turtle soup, but she had lost her appetite. Still clutching the basket of *baguettes*, she wandered off the gravel drive, into the stone yard.

Papa's stone yard had always been one of her favorite places. Light and shadow bounced off the marble shapes that lived in this garden of stone, each waiting to become something beautiful. She remembered, as a small child, playing hide-and-seek here with Armand. Now Cécile wondered about the children whose parents' names were etched into the stone markers inside Papa's workshop. Would they remember good times with their families, too? Or would they one day forget what it had been like to be in a family?

Cécile leaned against a great block of stone, shaded from the warm October sun. She listened as the clinking of tools in the workshop stopped and water splashed as the men washed off at the pump. She heard Grand-père's deep, gruff voice, probably telling a joke, and then Armand's laugh, louder than all the others. She heard Maman's soft murmurs, and the tinkle of spoons against bowls. Lunch was being served, but Cécile lingered in the shadows. She couldn't get the orphans out of her mind.

"Cécile!" It was her father's voice. She turned around. Papa had taken off his work smock, but the dust in his dark hair glinted in the sunlight.

"*Oui*, Papa?"

"Maman is looking for the bread, *chérie*." He reached to take her basket, but then he paused. He raised an eyebrow at her. "Are you all right?"

"I don't know, Papa," she said slowly. She told him about Perrine and about all the other orphans at Holy Trinity and Children of Mercy, whose lives would never be the same after this terrible summer. She tried to put words to the feelings in her heart. "Why . . . why do things have to change?"

Cécile tried to put words to the feelings in her heart.
"Why ... why do things have to change?" she asked.

Papa squatted down so that he could look into her eyes. Cécile stood very still.

"Everything must change, *ma petite*," Papa said. "Sometimes . . . we don't like it. Sometimes it hurts us, like this yellow fever that changed our family and many others. But change also makes us strong." He paused. "Sometimes it can make us strong enough to do important things."

Cécile could hardly believe it. But if Papa said this, it must be so. "Good things?" she asked.

"Oui. Great things." Papa smiled at her and stood up. It seemed to Cécile that her spirits lifted with him. Papa grasped her soft, small fingers inside his large, rough hand. "Now, come with me to the table. I'm starving!"

Cécile squeezed his hand and began to walk. She felt hopeful suddenly, as if a door had opened inside her mind.